The Robin's journey

Finding the perfect place to call Home

The little Robin was all grown,
He would make it on its own.
Leaving the safety of his parent's nest.
With a heavy heart and heavy chest.

Giving his parents a last goodbye.
Up he flew so high
He spread his wings and soared,
Soared through the sky.

He had a mission,
He had a plan,
Find my own new home, of course, I can.

He first found a place near the sky.
But it was too windy, much too high.
Upon a tree, on the highest branch,
But this was not a perfect match.

The second place was near the ground
Green and cozy, how does that sound?

But when he went inside,
he thought: this was not what I had in mind.
Getting stuck almost everywhere
Robin got quite a scare.

So up he went to someplace new,
He spread his wings and enjoyed the view

The third place was just right.
Not too dark, windy, or bright.
But the neighbours were way too chatty
for Robin much too loud and too tacky.

After another long chase
he found a pretty place
but for the summertime its much too cold
did he even see a little mould?

So up he went to someplace new,
spread his wings and flew.

A new place found and after a little investigating,
the Cat that kept on staring
jumped at Robin without hesitating.

Jumping up with a fright
Robin escaped the claws and terrifying paws
Every place seemed to have a flaw.

Robin landed at a cemetery
this place was quite legendary.
But even for him, it was just too spooky
For a new home it was far too gloomy.

So in the morning, he spread his wings,
a new search begins.

On his break, Robin realized
he would be searching no more.
A postbox near a wooden door.

It was just right.
It was not too high nor too low.
It was not too big nor too small.
It was even dry and warm.

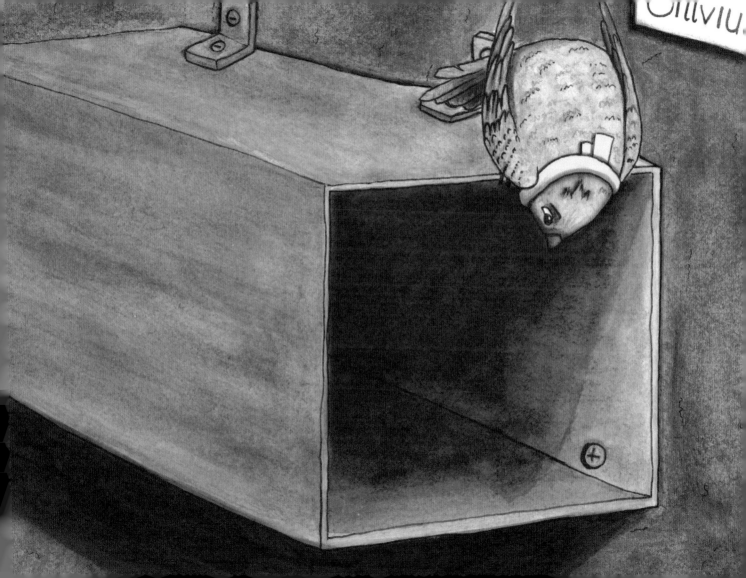

This will be the place! This will be my home!
He brought in new things,
Sticks, leaves, and many more twigs.

Something was weird
Something was off
All his sticks and twigs disappeared!

So he fought and fought with the lady that threw away his twigs.
He finally was able to convince.

The neighbours that at the beginning
had resisted,
Changed their mind quickly and visited.

Big blue, brown and green eyes
peeked inside
sometimes leaving even a snack behind.
But soon Robin didn't mind.

He finally finished his own nest,
The tale he could tell was an epic quest,
This place was now his own,
A wonderful little home.

Dedicated to the little red Robin that build
his home in our newspaper box,
who inspired me to write this story.

Even though it takes some time.
Never fret. When you spread your wings and fly
Fly through the sky
You will also find a place that you can call home.

Book written by Selina Zunino
with help of Shanara Zunino and Sally Bennek
Design and Formatting advices by Jonas Zechner.

Illustrated by Selina Zunino

ISBN: 9798584375430

Thank you to my Family and Friends that stood by me and helped me work through this wonderful Project.

Printed in Great Britain
by Amazon